WHERE DID TINY GO?

The Super Squad checked every possible hiding place —any place where a large, fat dog could get stuck. They looked under beds and in bathtubs. They opened dusty old rooms. They even checked the closets, where a dog might poke his nose and accidentally get locked in.

But there was no sign of Tiny.

Mr. Jenkins' face was very pale. "It's just not possible, girls," he said, "that Tiny has disappeared."

"And we've only got four hours until the dog show!" Marci cried.

THE MOST BEAUTIFUL DOG IN THE WORLD

Jennie Abbott
Illustrated by Mary Badenhop

Troll Associates

Library of Congress Cataloging in Publication Data

Abbott, Jennie.
    The most beautiful dog in the world.

    (The Super Squad)
    Summary: The Super Squad takes on a job getting a
large ugly dog ready for a dog show in hopes that he'll
win the title of "Most Beautiful Dog," only to have
him disappear right before the show.
    [1. Clubs—Fiction. 2. Dogs—Fiction] I. Badenhop,
Mary, ill. II. Title. III. Series.
PZ7.A156Mo   1988   [Fic]   87-14985
ISBN 0-8167-1187-9 (lib. bdg.)
ISBN 0-8167-1188-7 (pbk.)

A TROLL BOOK, published by Troll Associates,
Mahwah, NJ 07430

Printed in the United States of America.

10 9 8 7 6 5 4 3 2 1

THE MOST BEAUTIFUL DOG IN THE WORLD

Chapter 1

The Super Squad's weekly meeting wasn't a very happy affair. The four girls were wearing work clothes—jeans and T-shirts. But it didn't look as though there would be any work that afternoon. Marci Arnold rattled her papers, looking at her three best friends. The other girls sat around, staring glumly at the walls of the basement.

"I just don't know what to say," Marci finally admitted, glancing over her glasses. "We haven't had a job in four weeks. This isn't helping our Millionaire's Fund one bit." Since Marci's job was finding work and investing the pay for the Squad, this was bad news indeed.

"If this keeps up, I don't know why we should bother having meetings." Nicole Tucker's face grew sad and long. She put a dramatic hand to her forehead and let her dark hair fall forward to cover her face.

"Oh, no," Annie Lewis whispered to her friend Carrie Young. "Nicole's going to be depressed. You know how she gets. We've got to stop her."

"How do you do that?" Carrie whispered back. She gave her head an impatient shake, making her blond hair bounce.

"There must be some way to distract her," Annie said.

"Yeah," Carrie answered, "but we don't have any boys around here."

"Some other way," said Annie.

Right then, the phone rang.

"Could you answer that, Danny?" Marci called up to her younger brother.

"Why?" Danny yelled back.

"Because I'm bigger than you are. And if I have to come up there . . . "

"All right, all right!" Danny answered the phone on the fourth ring.

A second later, he grinned down at Marci from the top of the stairs. "It's for you."

Danny disappeared, and Marci ran upstairs. When she came back down, she was all smiles. "That was Mr. Jenkins from down the block. And what do you know?" she asked, not waiting for an answer. "He has a job for us."

"I'll bet it doesn't pay very well," Nicole said in a dreary voice.

"We'll get ten dollars a day," Marci answered.

"Ten dollars?" Nicole said, getting interested. Then she put her dreary voice on again. "I'll bet it's a crummy job."

"Ten dollars a day for ten days' work," said Marci. "That's a hundred dollars. And all we have to do is get his dog ready for the Riverview Dog Show."

Annie and Carrie looked at each other. "Why do I feel that this won't be as easy as she makes it sound?" Annie asked.

The next day, though, all four girls met at Mr. Jenkins's door. He had a big, white, old-fashioned wooden house, with green-painted shutters and a porch.

"Gee," said Marci as she rang the doorbell. "This place could do with a coat of paint. Maybe I could suggest—"

"Oh, no, not another painting job," Annie interrupted. "The last time, you had us working on a haunted house!"

"And Marci," said Carrie, "don't start bossing the poor man. Let's try and keep to one job at a time."

Mr. Jenkins answered the door. He was a tall, gray-haired man, stooped with age. But his eyes twinkled as he looked at the girls of the Super Squad.

"Well, young ladies," he said. "Right on time. I was having a cup of tea. Maybe you would like something, too. Milk? Cookies?"

"Oh, that sounds fine," said Nicole. She turned to Carrie and whispered, "I think I'm going to like this job."

Soon, all the girls were settled in big, fat armchairs with snacks. Marci looked around the living room. It was just the kind of room she'd have when she got rich. The big paintings on the walls, the dark wooden cases full of red leather books, the fireplace—even that dusty fur rug over in the corner—all were just perfect.

She sneaked another peek at the rug. She wondered what sort of animal it was, anyway. It seemed to be white. It could have been a polar bear. Too bad Mr. Jenkins had let it get so dusty. What the man really needed was someone to come in and clean things up for him. Could be another job in this, Marci noted. She'd store that piece of information in the back of her mind. . . .

Marci shook her head, realizing that Mr. Jenkins had been talking while her mind wandered.

". . . Several blue ribbons," Mr. Jenkins was saying. "Yes, Tiny is a champion dog. I've even entered him in the State Dog Show, and he won. That was some years ago, now."

Mr. Jenkins shook his head. "When I heard about the show here in town, I decided to put him up. Just for old times' sake." He looked a little worried. "I just hope it will be fair to the other animals—putting them up against a champion, I mean."

"Wow," said Nicole. "Tiny must be some dog."

"Oh, he is," said Mr. Jenkins. "But I think everything will be all right. Tiny is a bit out of shape. And getting him ready for the show will be a lot of work—too much for an old codger like me."

"Well, I guess that's where we come in." Marci rubbed her hands and looked very businesslike. "Counting today, we have ten days to prepare Tiny for the show."

"Exactly," said Mr. Jenkins. "Take him for walks. Get him used to being out among people again. I would hate to see him get skittish when the judges come around. You lose points for that, you know."

Marci nodded, although she had no idea. She'd have to have Annie brush up on the dog-show rules.

"And his fur may need a little trimming, of course," Mr. Jenkins continued. "And a bath and grooming before he goes to the show."

Annie and Carrie looked at each other. This really did seem like an easy job. It could even be fun!

"Well, I'll take him out for walks," Carrie volunteered. "I go out running almost everyday, anyway."

"And I can help with that trim," said Nicole. "I'm very good at doing people's hair."

"Well, you seem all set and ready to go. And you sound as if you'll enjoy your work. I bet I'm paying too much." He laughed at his little joke. "But then, where

Tiny is concerned, I'm happy to pay top dollar. You'll understand when you see him."

"What part of the Riverview Dog Show did you sign him up for?" Annie asked.

"There's only one prize for Tiny," Mr. Jenkins said firmly. "I signed him up for Most Beautiful Dog. He really is the handsomest animal I ever did see."

"I can hardly wait to meet him," Nicole said eagerly.

"Yes." Marci put down her empty glass and plate, and looked at her watch. "We should really be getting started."

"Fine. I'll call him." Mr. Jenkins got slowly to his feet. "Tiny," he called. "Tiny, come here."

From the corner of the room came a snort.

Marci and her friends all turned. And froze. That old fur rug in the corner had snorted and begun to move. Slowly, the grayish pile of fur pushed itself up onto four feet. It woofed and wagged its tail.

The girls sat still in their chairs, watching as the huge creature galumphed across the room to Mr. Jenkins.

Marci's chin dropped as she saw a big, pink tongue appear from the wild ball of dirty fur and lick Mr. Jenkins on the hand.

The elderly man smiled. "There you are, boy. Where have you been hiding?"

"Oh, no," she murmured. "*That's* Tiny?"

Chapter
2

Mr. Jenkins turned to the girls. He had a big smile on his face. "This is Tiny," he said proudly. "Go over and say hello to them, boy."

The Squad members stared in horror as Tiny waddled over to Marci. The huge dog put his head on her knee. He wagged his stubby tail as he looked up at her. His big, pink tongue lolled out. And he drooled all over the knee of her new jeans.

"Ooh, ick," said Nicole.

Tiny woofed and put a paw on Marci's leg. She was trapped in her seat. Tiny was one big dog. Looking at him closely, Marci realized there must be a sheepdog underneath all that fur. She figured Tiny had once been white, but now his fur was matted and gray with dirt. And he hadn't been cleaned for some time. "Whoo," Marci muttered, getting a whiff. Make that a long time.

Not only was the dog's fur tangled, but it had grown far too long. Tiny could hardly see where he was going because his hair had grown down over his eyes. In fact, in some places, it looked as if it had grown down to his chin.

He put another paw on Marci's leg and tried to climb up. "Yow! He's heavy!" she said. There must be a lot of fat under all that fur, she thought.

"D-Down, boy," she said.

"*This* is a champion?" Nicole said quietly. "He looks more like a mutt."

"How can we put him up for Most Beautiful Dog?" asked Annie.

"What's that?" Mr. Jenkins bent forward, putting his hand to his ear.

"We were thinking you might want to put Tiny up for some other award in the show," said Marci.

"Like what?" asked Mr. Jenkins.

"Um—how about Funniest Dog?" Annie suggested.

"Funny?" said Mr. Jenkins. "There's nothing funny about my Tiny." Two little red dots appeared in the old man's cheeks. He walked over to the bookcase. "That dog's a natural winner. I'll show you."

Mr. Jenkins pulled down an old leather album. "Look here," he said, opening the book.

Clipped to the page was a blue ribbon. "Best in Show," the faded gold letters read.

There were pictures on the page, too. They showed a fine, healthy sheepdog with a shiny coat of fur, standing proudly on a leash. Holding the leash was a much younger Mr. Jenkins.

The girls turned the pages, looking at more pictures of Tiny in his prime. There were several more blue ribbons, too.

"You see?" said Mr. Jenkins. "Tiny was a real show dog."

"Sure," whispered Annie. "Years ago."

Marci watched as Mr. Jenkins slowly bent over to pet Tiny's head. She saw the look in the old man's eyes. "Maybe so," she whispered back. "But Mr. Jenkins still thinks Tiny is the same beautiful dog he had then."

Suddenly Marci got very businesslike. "Well, we'd better start getting to work. We know what he looked like once. We'll just have to get him to look that way again."

Picking up one of the pictures from the album, she turned to Mr. Jenkins. "Could we borrow this, please?" she asked. "It will help us in fixing Tiny up."

"Of course," said Mr. Jenkins. "Is there anything else you need?"

Marci glanced over at Nicole. "We'll need some scissors, to give him a trim."

Nicole stared from Marci to Tiny's shaggy fur. "You expect me to go in and cut *that?*" she said.

"Right away," Marci said firmly. "Then he'll get a bath."

The Super Squad led Tiny outside while Mr. Jenkins went to get the necessary supplies.

"This is disgusting," Nicole complained as she

blew hair off her face. Not her hair. Tiny's. She stood in Mr. Jenkins's garden, working with a pair of scissors and a heavy brush, trimming back Tiny's fur. From time to time, she'd squint at the picture Marci held out.

"At least he holds still," Marci said.

Tiny did more than that. He lay down and promptly went to sleep.

"That big, lazy lump," Nicole said. "How am I supposed to trim the fur on his stomach if he's laying on it?" She gave Tiny a gentle shake. "Come on, boy, wake up. You have to roll over."

"Well, he looks cleaner with the dirty ends of his fur cut off," Marci said. "See how much whiter the fur underneath looks?"

Tiny finally gave a groan and rolled over.

"Oh, great," Nicole muttered as fresh dirt began to coat the newly cut fur.

"Just keep up the work on Step One," Marci said. "I'll go and help get things ready for Step Two." She walked over to Carrie and Annie, who were carrying a big tin washtub and a hose.

There was one thing about Tiny's haircut: With the hair out of his eyes, he could see a lot better. And when he saw that tub, he jumped to his feet.

"Hey!" said Nicole. "Where do you think you're going?"

She grabbed Tiny's collar, but he was as heavy as she was. When he tried to run away, he pulled her along, and Nicole landed face first onto a pile of dog hair.

"Ick-ick-ick!" she yelled, brushing frantically at her face.

Carrie began to laugh. "You look just like the monster in *Revenge of the Dog Girl*," she said.

"Very funny," said Nicole. "Why don't you run after that dog?"

Carrie set off, her long legs sprinting.

It wasn't a long chase. Tiny was so fat and out of shape, he didn't even get far. Soon, Carrie was leading him back, with a firm hand on his collar.

"Now," said Marci, "on to Step Two." They started filling the tub with water, pouring in some dog shampoo. A clean, soapy smell filled the air.

"Looks just like a bubble bath," Nicole said.

"Now all we have to do is get Tiny into it," said Carrie. She led the dog up to the tub. But about three feet away from it, Tiny stopped.

"Come on, Tiny," Carrie coaxed. "Look at the lovely bath we set up for you."

Tiny sat down.

"Let's go, Tiny." Carrie tugged at the dog's collar.

Tiny stuck out his paws and rested his head on them. Now he was completely lying down.

"Hey, Tiny. Up," said Carrie. "Up!" She pulled at Tiny's collar. But he flopped right down.

So did Carrie. "Whew!" she said, running a hand over her forehead. "It's like trying to pick up a truck!"

"C'mon, girls," Marci said. "Teamwork! I'll take this leg. Carrie, you take that one. Nicole, you take the one

19

opposite me. And Annie, you take the last one. We'll all lift together. One . . . two . . . three . . . now!''

They picked up the dog and staggered over to the tub.

"Wow!" Annie puffed as they walked. "He sure is heavy.''

"He's fat!" Nicole corrected her. "A real butterball.''

"Nicole, watch it!" Marci called out. "You're about to step in the tub!''

Nicole hopped around for a second, and the girls all teetered with the dog in their arms.

"Don't drop him!" Carrie said.

"Yeah. We'd never live through the splash!" said Nicole.

They finally steadied themselves, holding Tiny over the soapy water.

"Okay," said Marci. "Now we let him down. Gently . . . gently . . .''

They brought Tiny down. But as soon as he got near the water, he put his legs straight out. His paws got wet, but the water barely reached his belly.

"Come on, boy," Annie said. "Down. Feel the nice water? Down!''

"Dumb dog," muttered Nicole. "When you want him to get up, he lies down. When you want him to get down, he stands up.''

Carrie laughed. "I'd say he was a pretty smart dog.''

Tiny woofed in agreement.

"That's nice, but it's not getting Tiny into the water," Marci said. She put an experimental hand on Tiny's back. It was like trying to push a horse to its knees. She pushed on his rump, then gave him a gentle swat there. Tiny wiggled his behind, but he didn't sit.

"Keep an eye on him, girls," Marci said as she marched off into Mr. Jenkins's garage.

A few minutes later, she came back, carrying a big tin bucket. "So, you thought you could fake us out, huh?" she said, talking to Tiny.

She plunked the bucket down, squirted some shampoo into it, then got the hose. She bent over the bucket, squirting water. Suds foamed up. Marci's glasses slid down her nose, but she pushed them up with her free hand.

"Well, if we can't bring the dog to the water, we'll bring the water to the dog." She grunted, picking the bucket up. Then she walked over to the tub.

"See how you like this, Smart Guy," she said.

Slowly, she started spilling the water onto Tiny's back. Gently but thoroughly, she made sure all of him was covered, except for his head. "We'll take care of his face last," Marci said. "I don't want to get any of this shampoo in his eyes."

She grinned down at the now sopping wet dog. "So, in spite of your fighting, there you are. What do you think about that?"

Tiny began to quiver.

Carrie's eyes got big. "Look out!" she yelled. "He's going to . . ."

But it was too late. Before any of the girls could move, Tiny gave a great shake.

Chapter
3

The members of the Super Squad were sitting in Marci's basement again. This time they were wearing borrowed robes, towels, and blankets. Their clothes were tumbling in the Arnolds' dryer.

Marci looked at her friends. "Well," she said defiantly, "we gave Tiny his bath."

"Yeah," said Nicole. "And then *he* gave us a shower." She fluffed her hair in annoyance. "He ruined my new hair style," she pouted.

"I hate to say it," Annie said, "but this job may be too much for us."

"What?" Marci exclaimed. "I don't believe I'm hearing this. We have ten days to fix Tiny up. And look how far we've come, just today."

"Right," Nicole said. "Before we went to work, he was fat and sloppy. Now he's just fat."

"See? We're halfway there already," Marci said confidently. "And you know what got us there? Teamwork!"

"Sure," Carrie muttered. "Like how we all carried him to the tub?"

"No, I mean putting our best talents to work," Marci said. "The way Nicole trimmed back his fur." She thought a second. "Or the way Carrie ran to catch him when he tried to get away."

"But what other talents can we use?" Annie asked. "We only have nine days left to get Tiny ready for that dog show. And none of us has a magic wand to turn Tiny back into a young champion again."

"No, but I've got a computer. And Dad is friendly with Dr. Meechum, the veterinarian. I'll figure out a diet to help him slim down a little. And Carrie will be taking him out for exercise." She turned to Annie. "We need to know more about dog grooming—and about this dog show. Could you check into it?"

Annie nodded. "Sure."

"We all know Tiny is a champion," Marci continued. "He's just forgotten how to act like one. So it's up to us to remind him." She looked around the room with a big smile. "By the time the show comes around, I bet he'll love all the stuff we're doing."

The other girls didn't seem so sure.

"I hope you're right, Marci," Carrie finally said. "But I wouldn't go betting the Millionaire's Fund on it."

Of course, Carrie turned out to be right. Marci found that out the next afternoon.

"Phone, Marci," her father called. He had finished teaching his course at the university and was home early. "It's Carrie."

Marci turned off the computer and picked up the phone. "What's going on?" she asked. "You're supposed to be out walking Tiny." Behind her glasses, her eyes squinted with suspicion. "You're not stuck late at some practice, are you?" Carrie was always practicing at some sport or other.

"No, I'm not." Carrie sounded very upset.

"Then where are you?"

"You know that little police station at the park?" Carrie said miserably. "That's where I am."

"And Tiny?" Loud barking in the background answered Marci's question almost as she asked it.

Then what Carrie was saying finally sank in. "The *police* station? What are you doing there?"

"We're in trouble," Carrie said. "You know that diet you started Tiny on? I don't think he likes it."

"Well, it's good for him," Marci said. "And it's nutritious."

"Maybe so, but I think it makes him very hungry."

"How do you know?" Marci asked defensively.

"Because of what Tiny did today at the park," Carrie said. "We were out running when he spotted this family having a picnic. Well, he pulled me over to them, and then. . . ."

"And then what?" Marci wanted to know.

"And then he ate their sandwiches—all of them. Right out of their picnic basket, Marci! Well, of course, they complained to the police, and here I am."

"Carrie!" Marci cried, horrified. "That wasn't on his diet! How could you let him do something like that?"

"I didn't let him." Carrie was getting hysterical. "He pulled me over there. It was like trying to stop a truck. Then he got his nose in the picnic basket and started chomping away—" Carrie suddenly stopped. "And what about me?" she wailed. "I'm in trouble. My parents aren't home yet. And you're more interested in your stupid diet!"

Marci blinked. "Um, you're right. I'll get help. We'll be down there right away."

She hung up the phone. "Oh, Dad," she called. "Want to take me for a ride?"

The drive back from the police station was quiet. Dangerously quiet. "I had to pay for new sandwiches for those people," Mr. Arnold muttered as he drove along. "All nine of them. Do you know what that cost?"

"I said we'd pay you back, Dad," Marci said from the back seat. Beside her Tiny lay sprawled out, looking very pleased with himself. "As soon as we get home, I'll pay you from the Millionaire's Fund."

"Fine. First, we'll drop Carrie off." Carrie sat in the front seat beside Mr. Arnold. She was still shaking. "And then you'll get rid of that dog."

"What?" said Marci. "No, we can't do that, Dad. He still has to get his exercise."

Carrie turned around in her seat. "Marci, are you crazy? That dumb dog almost got me arrested! And you heard that policeman. I'm not allowed to bring Tiny into the park again because I couldn't control him."

"We'll just have to come up with a new route for him to run along," Marci said. "One that doesn't take us near the park—or anybody with sandwiches."

"I agree with your dad. I think we should just give up on Tiny," Carrie said. "Tell Mr. Jenkins . . ."

"Tell him what?" Marci asked. "That the dog he loves isn't a champion anymore? That he's a big, fat bum?"

Tiny lifted up his head and whined.

"Besides," Marci went on, "that would mean we'd lose money on the deal. We wouldn't get paid." She grinned in spite of herself. "And we'd still owe all that money for those sandwiches."

The Squad gathered later in the afternoon in Mr. Jenkins's yard. Carrie and Marci tried to get Tiny to do a little exercise.

But Tiny had other plans. He trotted over to a spot of bare earth by the garden, rolled in the dirt, then lay down for a snooze.

"Well," said Nicole, "if we're going to make this dumb mutt do anything, we'll have to outthink him." She reached into her pocket and opened a little plastic bag.

"Oh, Tiny," she called, holding out her hand.

Tiny's nose twitched and his ears flapped. He got up, his tail wagging.

"What have you got there?" Marci asked, coming over.

"It's a doggy treat. They're Tiny's favorite food—I asked Mr. Jenkins." Nicole smiled. "Of course, you took them off his diet."

"Then why are you holding one out to him?" Marci asked.

"I've got an idea. If we get him to exercise and give him just one, that won't hurt his diet too much, will it?"

Marci shrugged. "I guess not."

"So I bet I can get him to do stuff by showing him the doggy treat." Nicole walked over to Tiny and held the dog biscuit high over her head. "Okay, Tiny," she said. "Jump for it. Come now, jump!"

Tiny jumped. But he came nowhere near the doggy treat. His front paws landed on Nicole's shoulders and knocked her right down.

"Yikes!" Nicole cried as she tumbled into the dirt. The doggy treat she was holding flew out of her hand.

Tiny leaped, caught it in midair, and happily crunched the treat in his jaws.

29

Nicole got up, shaking her head. "Oh, no," she wailed. "That's the second hair style that dumb mutt has ruined," she complained, fluffing out her hair.

"Yes, but you did show us something," Marci said.

"What?" Nicole wanted to know.

"He did jump to get the doggy treat," Marci pointed out. "And when it went flying, he jumped again to get it. That's the most I've ever seen him do."

"Great," said Annie. "We knew he loved to eat. And now we know his favorite food."

"We know he'll do things to get doggy treats," Marci said. "If someone ran ahead of him with one, I bet he'd run after them."

"Yeah," said Nicole. She gave Tiny a dark look. "Run after them, knock them down, and eat the stupid thing."

"That is, if he didn't find someone with sandwiches along the way," Carrie added. She gave Tiny an angry look, too.

"We'll just have to fix things so he can't do that." Marci leaned forward. "I've got an idea. . . ."

When Tiny set out to run again, it looked like a parade. Carrie ran in front, holding out a doggy treat. Then Tiny came galumphing along. Marci ran behind him, holding tightly onto his leash. On Tiny's left side ran Annie, and on his right, Nicole. Whenever

31

Tiny started veering to one side or the other, they helped Marci get him back on course.

Tiny might be a lazy dog, but he was also a stubborn one. When he saw and sniffed the doggy treat in front of him, he was going to get it—or bust. But from the way he was puffing, it might be bust, after all.

"Carrie, do we have to run so fast?" Marci asked. "I don't know if Tiny can keep this up."

She stumbled as Tiny tried to dart to one side, making a leap for the treat.

"I don't know." Carrie grinned. "Are you worried for Tiny? Or for yourself?"

Marci stopped running. "Just because I'm a little out of breath—"

The rest of her answer was lost as she went staggering forward, pulled by Tiny's leash.

"Come on," Annie encouraged her friend. "Just keep your mind on the money we're earning by doing all this."

"Yeah," said Nicole. "Think of how you can invest it. Anyway, we'll be finished soon." She looked at Carrie hopefully. "Won't we?"

"We'll just go to the end of this field," Carrie called. "You know what? I do believe Tiny is beginning to like this." She ran a little faster, opening a gap between herself and Tiny.

Tiny gave a loud bark and bounded forward, once again in pursuit.

"Oh, great," Marci muttered as she ran to keep up with Tiny. "I'm glad *someone* is enjoying this."

Chapter
4

Over the next few days, Tiny really began to show signs of improvement. As Annie began to practice grooming him, he stopped taking his daily rolls in the dirt. He'd lie quietly in Mr. Jenkins's garden, waiting for the girls to arrive.

When they'd come in through the gate, he'd get to his feet and frolic with them for a few minutes before getting down to work. "Hey, Tiny!" they would call. Tiny would bound through the air in a clumsy somersault.

As the week went on, the somersault became less and less clumsy. Tiny didn't puff as much on his daily runs, either. His coat began to shine—both from Annie's work and from his daily exercise.

Marci felt proud of all their work as she watched

Annie practicing with Tiny. She was taking him slowly around the garden, trying to get him to walk like a show dog.

Tiny was much more used to throwing himself around. But as Annie patiently marched with him, his half-remembered training began to take hold. Tiny held his head high, carefully placing his feet as he walked along.

Marci smiled. Tiny almost looked like the dog in Mr. Jenkins's pictures. "Except that he's fatter," Marci said with a smile.

Just then Tiny tripped over his feet and fell down.

"And a lot more clumsy," she added.

Tiny whimpered as he got back to his feet.

"He's not hurt, is he?"

"Oh, he's all right," Annie answered. "He just hates to do something wrong." She grinned. "I think he's starting to get some of his old pride back."

Tiny barked and pulled on his leash. He and Annie marched all the way around the garden without an accident. Then the big dog stopped and wagged his tail proudly.

Carrie came up, looking at her watch. "It's about time for our run," she said.

Tiny's ears came up. He barked, then did another somersault.

The girls took their usual positions. Even though Tiny was behaving much better, they didn't want to take chances.

They opened the garden gate, and Carrie set off down the road, holding out the doggy treat. Tiny bounded off in pursuit. The girls ran to keep up. They ran for several blocks, until they came to a big, grassy field at the edge of town.

"Okay, here we go," said Carrie. "To the edge of the field, and then back again!"

Every other day they had come to the field, it had been empty. Today, though, they could see four boys running and jumping across the grass.

"What are those guys doing?" Nicole asked. Interest gleamed in her eyes. She whipped out a small mirror and checked her hair. Satisfied, she closed it again.

The boys appeared to be leaping and hopping around as they ran.

"Don't pay any attention to them," Marci puffed, knowing her friend's weakness for boys. "We've got a job to do."

The girls probably should have paid attention to them, however. Because as the Super Squad (and Tiny) bounded along, the boys came leaping and running right ahead of them.

"Look out!" Carrie yelled. A good-looking boy was in midleap in front of her. She jumped to one side, and Tiny, still chasing his doggy treat, went after her.

Marci, still holding onto the leash, wound up on the other side of the boy. The leash caught the boy right around the knees. Marci flew around in a half circle. So did Tiny. Between the two of them, they pulled the leash completely around the boy's legs. He toppled over like a cut-down tree.

Another boy appeared, with dark hair, and a video camera in his hand. He zoomed in on the fallen boy, who was trying to get loose from the leash—and from Tiny who was licking him.

"Cut!" the dark-haired boy hollered, standing up. "That was great, Bobby. How did you know the dog was going to do that?"

By this time, Bobby was sitting up. "I didn't know, Tommy," he said, finally getting free from the leash. "I just didn't see the dog coming. If I had, I would've gotten out of the way." He ducked as Tiny came forward to lick him again.

"Well, it's going to look great in the video," Tommy said.

"Video?" said Marci. "What's going on?"

"Oh, uh, nothing," Bobby said. "We're just trying out the camera."

"We're making a music video," Tommy said. The other two boys had come over and were looking at the girls. "What were you girls doing?"

"Walking the dog," Marci explained.

"Four of you to walk one dog?" Bobby was standing now, running a hand through his light-brown hair. His blue eyes twinkled as he looked down at Tiny. "But I can see why. He's a pretty big dog."

36

"His name's Tiny," Marci said. "I'm Marci Arnold, and these are my friends." She introduced Annie, Carrie, and Nicole.

"I'm Bobby McCann," Bobby said. "And this is Tommy Mills, Dennis Page, and Joe Moore. We're—"

"Loud Noise!" Nicole suddenly spoke up. "I thought you guys looked familiar. We all saw you playing at this year's pep rally. You've got a really great band."

"Hey, thanks," said Tommy, smiling at Nicole. "We're going to be playing at the school dance this Saturday. I hope all of you will be coming to hear us."

"Oh, yeah!" said Nicole.

"Sure," said Carrie.

"You bet." Annie grinned.

"I'm sorry we ruined your video," Marci said to Bobby.

"No, it's my fault," Bobby answered. "I should have watched where I was going and not bumped into you like that."

"Besides," Tommy cut in, "you didn't ruin the video. That fall was the funniest part yet."

"Look, we were just finishing filming," Bobby said. "Now we're going to practice for a while at my house. I live right near here. Would you like to come and hear us play?"

"*Would* we?" Nicole said dreamily.

"We'd love to," Marci spoke up, "as soon as we finish Tiny's exercise. We have to run from one end of the field to the other. Can you wait until then?"

"Sure." Bobby smiled at her. "We'll just get our stuff together and get out of the way."

Marci grinned back at him. "Great." She turned to the girls. "Well, let's get going!"

They raced back and forth across the field. Then they followed the members of Loud Noise to Bobby's house.

"Our instruments are all set up in the basement," Bobby explained. "Right down these stairs."

"What do you play?" Marci asked as she followed Tiny down the stairway. The big dog pulled on his leash, eagerly sniffing the strange room.

"I play drums," Bobby said, turning on the lights. "Joe's our lead guitarist, Dennis is on bass, and Tommy plays the keyboards."

"I can hardly wait to hear you," Nicole said, looking around the room. She batted her eyelashes at Tommy and smiled. "Where do you want us to sit?"

The basement was pretty cramped with the band's setup. And a big pool table stood in the middle of the room, taking up more space.

Bobby walked around his drums. "You can sit on this couch by the wall," he said, leading the girls over. "That way you can hear us, but you won't be too close." He smiled at Marci. "We have to play pretty loud sometimes."

Marci smiled again. "I guess that's how you got your name," she said.

She asked Bobby lots of questions about Loud Noise—

39

where they played, what songs they liked to do. He told a couple of funny stories about the band. Somewhere along the way, she let go of Tiny's leash.

Joe had turned on his amplifier, and a loud, buzzing hum filled the room. He plugged in his guitar and began to tune it up.

Tiny, hearing the hum, tracked it down. He stood in front of the amp, poking his nose at it. Then Joe hit his strings. A loud chord came out of the amp. Tiny jumped back—right into Bobby's drum set. THUMP! went the bass drum. KEEEE-RASSSSSHHHH! went the cymbals.

"Yipe, yipe, yipe!" went Tiny, trying to get away from this new noise. Instead, he blundered into a rack of pool cues standing by the pool table. They swayed for a second, then went clattering to the floor.

Nicole turned from where she was talking with Tommy. "Oh, Tiny," she wailed. "How could you?"

Marci jumped up. "Is everything okay? We'll help fix things up. Nothing's broken, is it? We'll pay for anything that got broken!"

"Why is she babbling on like that?" Carrie asked Annie in a whisper.

"And she's offering to spend money. She *never* offers to spend money," Annie whispered back. "What's going on, here?"

"Oh, don't worry," said Bobby as he picked up his cymbals. "See? They're not even dented."

Marci turned from where she was picking up the pool

40

cues. "I'm very sorry," she said. "Maybe we should go."

Bobby looked disappointed. "Please stay," he said. "You haven't heard us play, yet."

"Yeah," said Nicole, smiling at Tommy.

"Well, if you really want us," Marci said. "I promise I'll hold onto Tiny's leash."

They sat back down as the boys got ready. Then Bobby called out, "A-one, a-two. A-one, two, three!" The boys started playing.

Marci and her friends started bouncing on the sofa, moving in time to the beat. "They're really good!" Nicole shouted over the music.

"They're wonderful!" Marci agreed.

The only one who wasn't enjoying the music was Tiny. He cowered at the foot of the couch, scared by the loud noise.

Finally, he sat up, threw back his head, and let out a long, frightened howl.

Tiny was a big dog, with big lungs. His howl even drowned out Loud Noise's music. Bobby stopped playing. So did Tommy. Then Dennis stopped. Only Joe went on for a few notes before realizing that nobody else was playing, then stopped.

In the sudden silence, Tiny howled again.

"He's scared," Annie said. "Look at the way he's shaking."

"Maybe we should go," Marci mumbled. "I'm sorry Tiny is being so much trouble."

"We don't mind. Do we, guys?" Bobby looked at the other band members.

"Of course not," said Tommy. "Why don't you bring Tiny upstairs? Then the music won't be loud enough to scare him."

"Good idea!" said Bobby. "I was going to go up and get some sodas, anyhow." He reached over for Tiny's leash.

"Are you sure that's a good idea?" Marci asked anxiously. "I mean, you saw what he did down here."

"We don't have anything out in the kitchen," Bobby assured her. "We've got a dog, too. There's a gate in the kitchen, so Tiny won't be able to go anywhere else. Why don't you come up and see?"

He took Tiny's leash. "Come on, boy."

Tiny was only too glad to leave the room.

Marci followed them up the stairs and into the kitchen. Bobby was right. There was nothing out in the kitchen.

"Bucky ate already, so her bowl is away," Bobby said. He glanced out the window. "I guess she's out in the back yard."

"How does she get out?" Marci asked. Then she saw the flap built into the kitchen door. It was very small. "What kind of dog is Bucky, anyway?" she asked.

"A Chihuahua," said Bobby. "Do you think Tiny would like some water?"

Tiny's ears went up and he whined.

Marci laughed. "I guess so."

They left Tiny happily lapping up some water from a bowl, and carried down eight cans of soda.

The band started practicing again, running through three songs they knew, and then working on a new one. The girls really enjoyed themselves. Marci kept a careful ear out for any more howling. But everything was quiet upstairs.

Then, as Joe practiced a particularly tough set of chords alone, Marci heard something.

"Ra-ra-ra-ra-RA!" Squeaky barking burst out from the kitchen. Then it stopped for a second. Then, *"Ra-ra-ra-ra-RA!"* burst out again.

"Bucky's back!" Bobby said.

"Who knows what Tiny is up to?" Marci exclaimed.

Together, they raced up the stairs.

"Ra-ra-ra-ra-RA!"

They burst into the kitchen and stopped in their tracks.

Bucky stood by the water bowl. Tiny lay down in the middle of the kitchen floor, with his paws over his face. Bucky leaned over the bowl and lapped up a little water. Whenever Tiny tried to move, Bucky would whirl around. *"Ra-ra-ra-ra-RA!"* she'd go, and Tiny would cower down again.

Bobby began to laugh. "Well, it looks as if Tiny found out who's boss in this house," he said.

Marci laughed, too. Then she stopped when she got a look at the clock on the wall. "It's getting late," she said. "We really should be heading home now."

"Well, if you have to go, you have to go," said Bobby. "Remember the dance on Saturday. And maybe I'll see you before then."

As they walked home, all the girls were smiling.

"That was fun!" Annie said.

"Yeah, who'd have thought we'd meet the guys from Loud Noise," said Carrie.

"*And* get invited to the dance." Nicole sighed. "That Tommy is really nice."

"So is Bobby," Marci added. She remembered the way Bobby had smiled at her. His wavy, light-brown hair. Those deep-blue eyes, and the way they twinkled when he laughed. He really was good-looking. And nice.

Then she saw the other three girls were all looking at her. "Now I think I know why Marci was acting funny," Annie said. "I think she's in love!"

Marci turned bright red. "I am not!" she said. "Come on, Tiny!"

Together, they ran the last few blocks to Mr. Jenkins's house.

Chapter 5

With just one day to go before the Riverview Dog Show, the Super Squad had every reason to be proud. They had done a fine job with Tiny.

As they took him out for his daily run, he looked every inch a champion. His coat was neatly trimmed and glossy. And even though he was still fatter than his old self, he looked fit and healthy.

"We really outdid ourselves this time," Marci said. "Aren't you glad now that we didn't give up on this job?"

Annie, Carrie, and Nicole had to agree.

"It really turned out perfect," Marci said. Almost, she added to herself. There was one thing that wasn't finished satisfactorily. Bobby. Well, he wasn't really part of the job, Marci reminded herself. Even if she had met him while she was working.

She was really looking forward to the dance on Saturday night. As soon as the dog show was finished, she was going to start getting ready.

Even now, as they came up on the big field, she looked around anxiously. Bobby had said he might see her before the dance. But this would be the last day. . . .

A smile grew on her face as she saw two familiar figures standing in the field. One was Tommy. The other was Bobby! He was holding a piece of rope or something that dragged down into the long grass. When he saw the Super Squad, he waved his free hand.

"Let's go over and say hello," Marci said.

"Yeah!" said Nicole eagerly. She quickly smoothed her mint-green blouse.

"Sure, sure." Annie began to giggle.

"Hi, Bobby," Marci called. All of a sudden, she felt very shy.

"Hi," said Bobby. He grinned as Tiny woofed a hello.

"Ra-ra-ra-ra-RA!" came an answer from the tall grass. Bucky burst into view, pulling on her leash. Tiny got down on his forepaws until he was nose to nose with the little Chihuahua.

Everyone laughed. "They look so silly!" Marci said.

Bobby grinned at her. "I wondered if I would bump into you again," he said. "Whenever I took Bucky for a walk, I kept an eye out for you and your dog."

"Oh, he's not my dog," Marci said.

"But I thought—" Bobby shook his head. "I guess he belongs to one of your friends, then."

"Guess again," said Carrie.

"We're the Super Squad, and we do odd jobs," Marci explained. "Tiny is one of them. We're getting him ready for the Riverview Dog Show tomorrow."

"No fooling?" said Bobby. "That's funny. I've entered Bucky in the show."

"Maybe we'll see you there before the dance," Marci said. "We're going to give Tiny a final grooming tomorrow morning. Then he's going to win the Most Beautiful Dog contest."

"Really?" said Tommy. He looked thoughtfully from Tiny to Bucky.

"That's right," Carrie picked up the story. "Tiny's an old hand at winning dog shows. When he was young, he got all sorts of blue ribbons. But when we first saw him, he looked like El Grosso!"

"He was dirty, and lazy, and his fur was all over the place!" Nicole explained. "We've cleaned him up and gotten him all ready. Mr. Jenkins is sure to win."

"See how smart he is!" said Nicole, turning to Tiny. "Hey, Tiny," she said.

Immediately, Tiny did his somersault.

"Great," said Tommy. But he didn't look pleased.

Bobby looked at his watch. "Hey, I've got to be going. See you soon." He gave a little jerk on his leash and led Bucky away.

"Yeah," said Tommy. "See you."

"We'll be there at the dance," Nicole called after him.

But Marci noticed that Bobby didn't smile at her as he left. And Tommy seemed upset. What's the matter with them? she wondered.

Then Carrie started running again, and Tiny set off after her. Marci needed all of her attention to keep from being tripped or pulled flat.

When they got back from their run, Annie let Tiny cool off. Then she gave him one more brushing down. "This should be it until tomorrow," she said. "We should get here early in the morning. He'll need a B-A-T-H." She spelled out the letters so Tiny wouldn't understand.

Nicole grinned. "If it's anything like the last time, we'd better bring our old clothes."

"We'll have to change afterward, then," Carrie said. "Before going to the show." She looked at her friends. "We are going, aren't we? I mean, it would be like watching the team practice all week and not going to see the big game."

Marci laughed. "You're exactly right, Carrie. Look, everybody can bring stuff over to my house. We can change there after we're finished with Tiny."

Tiny heard his name and gave a questioning woof from where he lay by the garden.

Everybody laughed. The talk went on to what they would wear for the dog show—and then, what they would wear to the school dance afterward.

"This is going to be great!" Nicole hugged herself

with excitement. "I think Tommy likes me."

"You *always* think somebody likes you," Annie said. "I'm more interested in Bobby McCann. Or maybe I should say, I think somebody here likes him."

Marci found herself blushing furiously. She didn't know what to say. Luckily, Mr. Jenkins came out onto the porch just then. Tiny popped up and trotted over to his master. He nudged Mr. Jenkins's hand with his nose. The old man gently patted Tiny's long, silky coat.

"He certainly looks fine, girls. Like a real champion."

Tiny leaned his head back. He stood proudly. Then his big, pink tongue lolled out of his mouth.

"Well, pretty much like a real champion." Carrie laughed.

But Mr. Jenkins just beamed fondly down at his dog. "Yes, he looks just as he did in the good old days."

Mr. Jenkins straightened up then and reached into his pocket. "You've done a splendid job," he said. "I appreciate it very much. And now I'd like to pay you what I owe—"

"Not yet, Mr. Jenkins," Marci said. "We have some last-minute stuff to take care of tomorrow, before the show. For one thing"—she leaned her head closer to Mr. Jenkins—"he's going to need a B-A-T-H."

Mr. Jenkins laughed when he heard that. "You're right. We don't want to go giving him any warning about that."

"And then, Annie wants to do a final grooming. You can pay us after that."

Mr. Jenkins smiled down at Marci. "I can't thank you enough. But I want to let you know how much we appreciate it—both Tiny and myself."

Tiny barked in agreement.

Mr. Jenkins laughed as he called Tiny over. "Now Tiny is going to have one of your famous dinners. And we'll rest up for the big day tomorrow. Goodbye. I'll see you tomorrow morning."

The dog and the old gentleman walked into the house. The Super Squad waved good-bye and headed for the garden gate.

Marci was up early the next morning. She was just too excited to sleep. There was so much to do to get Tiny ready for the dog show. She wondered if she'd see Bobby there.

"I wonder in what event he entered Bucky?" she said to her reflection as she brushed her wavy brown hair. "I should have asked him yesterday. There's just so much going on!" She put her glasses on and gave one final look in the mirror.

After the dog show, there was the school dance. She wondered how that would turn out. She had carefully bought a new dress just for the occasion. She was looking forward to the dance, but was nervous at the same time. She wanted to look her best for Bobby.

"Well, I'm not going to think about it anymore," she stated as she pulled on a T-shirt and a pair of tan shorts. "There's work to be done."

She ran downstairs and had breakfast. Then she sat outside, waiting for the other Super Squad members to show up.

Annie and Carrie arrived, carrying the outfits they'd wear for the dog show. Then Nicole arrived with her outfit, rubbing sleep from her eyes.

"I *hate* having to get up early on Saturdays," she grumbled. "It's the one day I really get to sleep."

Marci laughed when she saw her friend had pulled her hair back in a ponytail. "Well, this morning you're going to spend giving a dog a bath. And it looks like you've figured out just the hair style for it!"

All the girls laughed and set off down the block to Mr. Jenkins's place. They opened the garden gate and braced themselves. But Tiny didn't come bounding up to greet them.

They looked over to the patch of grass by the garden where Tiny usually waited for them. But he wasn't there either.

"Hey, Tiny," Carrie called. She looked around. "Where could he be?"

"Uh-oh," said Annie, with a grin. "You don't think he can spell, do you? Maybe he realized we'd be giving him a bath—so he's hiding."

"Don't be silly," Marci said. "We always come to work on Tiny in the afternoon. Maybe he spends his mornings inside with Mr. Jenkins."

She walked up onto the porch and rang the bell.

Mr. Jenkins answered the door with a big smile. "Well, well, all here, bright and early!"

"Mr. Jenkins, is Tiny inside with you?" Marci asked.

The old man looked surprised. "Why, no," he said. "I let him out into the garden after breakfast." He stepped onto the porch. "Tiny!" he called. Mr. Jenkins walked into the garden. "Tiny! Here, boy!" he called again.

The girls followed him as he walked all the way around the house, searching.

"I can't understand it," Mr. Jenkins said, shaking his head. "Unless he came back inside while I wasn't watching." He led the way back to the porch and into the house.

They checked the kitchen and Tiny's doggy dish. They went into the living room to check the warm spot by the window where he liked to lie down. They checked the basket where he slept. No Tiny.

Mr. Jenkins became more and more worried. "We'll search the house," he said. "Floor by floor, and room by room, if necessary."

For the next half-hour, they checked every possible hiding place—any possible place where a large, fat dog could get stuck. They looked under beds and into bathtubs. They opened dusty old rooms, where the furniture was kept under sheets. They checked under those sheets, too. They even checked the closets, where

a dog might poke his nose and accidentally get locked in.

But still, there was no sign of Tiny.

Mr. Jenkins was mopping his forehead with a hand-kerchief. His face was very pale. "It's just not possible, girls," he said, "but it seems to have happened. Tiny has disappeared!"

Chapter
6

"Disappeared?" said Carrie.

"Oh, no!" said Nicole.

"What are we going to do?" asked Annie.

"Has he ever done this before?" Marci forced herself to remain calm.

Mr. Jenkins shook his head. "Tiny has been with me for ten years, and he's never run away before."

"Well, we'll just have to find him!" Marci said. "It's nine o'clock. We still have four hours until the Riverview Dog Show begins." She thought for a moment. "When was the last time you saw Tiny?"

"About half an hour before you girls arrived," said Mr. Jenkins. "I let him out right after breakfast."

"Then he couldn't have gone too far. We'll look around the neighborhood first. Then we'll go along the route we take for our walks. He's used to going that way."

"Shall I come with you?" Mr. Jenkins asked.

"I think you should stay here," Marci suggested. "In case Tiny comes back."

Mr. Jenkins nodded. "You're right. Well, I'll be here, waiting for you. Good luck, girls!"

He waved good-bye as the girls hurried out the garden gate. He looked a lonely and worried figure.

"Where do we start?" Carrie asked.

"First, we'll go around the block," Marci said. "He might just have wandered away."

They walked around the block, calling, "Here, Tiny! Tiny, where are you? Come on, boy!"

Suddenly, the upstairs window of one of the houses flew up. "Quiet!" a voice shouted. "There are people still trying to sleep around here!"

Annie looked at her friends. "Tiny!" she whispered. "Where are you?"

Carrie shook her head. "I don't think that's going to work."

"What do we do now?" Nicole wanted to know.

"If we can't call, we'll just have to look—and ask," said Marci. She went up to the next yard, peeking over the fence.

"I don't see him here," she said.

They headed to the next house. A man was outside, mowing the lawn.

"Excuse me," Marci said. "Did you see a big, white

dog pass by here? A sheepdog?''

The man shook his head. Marci continued on.

They circled the block without finding Tiny. Then they moved onto the next block, and the next.

''We're getting nowhere,'' Marci finally said. ''Let's try our route out to the field.''

They started off, but still no trace of Tiny.

''I wish we knew he went this way,'' Carrie said. ''We could be wasting our time.''

Marci saw a woman walking by with a shopping cart.

''Excuse me.'' The question was becoming a habit. ''Have you seen a white sheepdog passing here?'' Also by habit, she started moving along.

''Why, yes,'' the woman said. ''I think so.''

Marci stopped. ''You think so?'' she repeated.

''I was outside the supermarket, loading my wagon,'' the woman explained. ''I did get a glimpse of a large, white, fluffy dog while I was bent over.'' She shrugged. ''But I was more interested in my groceries than I was in dogs, just then.''

''Did you notice which way the dog was going?'' Marci asked hopefully.

''That way,'' the woman said, pointing back the way she'd come.

''And you saw the dog by Redfern's Super Foods?'' Marci asked.

''That's right,'' said the woman. ''I wouldn't have even looked, but I heard a voice saying, 'Come on, fella. Come on!'''

"Oh," said Annie. "He was with someone. Then it mustn't be our dog. He's out by himself. That's why we're looking for him."

"But how many sheepdogs could there be around here?" Marci questioned. "Maybe somebody found Tiny wandering around and took him."

She thanked the lady, then headed down the street. "I'm going to Redfern's to ask around. It's our only clue so far."

They reached the supermarket and began asking people if they'd seen a sheepdog. But no one had.

"Well, that lady said they kept going along our route," said Carrie. "Let's follow along. Maybe we'll find someone else who saw them."

They continued along until they passed a big, wooden house. An elderly woman knelt outside on the grass, working on her garden. She had often waved to the girls as they passed by with Tiny. So the girls stopped to ask if she'd seen him coming by.

"You don't have your dog today," the woman said, smiling, before Marci could even ask her question.

"No, ma'am," said Nicole. "Today we're looking for him. We think he ran away."

"We thought maybe he came by here," Marci said. "Have you seen him?"

The woman nodded. "I did see a big dog like yours, just a little while ago. In fact, he must have been yours. He had no leash, and the boy he was with had to hold onto his collar."

"Boy?" said Nicole, looking interested.

"He was with a boy?" said Annie.

"What did the boy look like?" asked Marci.

"He was the nice boy who always helps carry my packages from Redfern's," said the lady. "I'm afraid I don't know his name. He's always whistling. A very nice boy."

The woman frowned in thought for a moment. "As I recall, he is in a band with his friends. Once, he even invited me to hear them play. Imagine that!" The old woman chuckled to herself.

"Oh, it has to be Bobby!" Marci said. "Thanks very much, ma'am. You've helped us a lot!"

She led the way as the four of them rushed for the field. "I bet Bobby found Tiny near the super-market," Marci said as she ran. "He knew who he was, so he grabbed the collar. But he doesn't know where we live! So he took Tiny to the field. He'll be waiting there for us!"

But when they reached the field, there wasn't a soul in sight. No Bobby. No Tiny. Just lots and lots of green grass.

"Maybe he took Tiny to his house," Carrie suggested.

"You're right!" Marci exclaimed. "Bobby doesn't know where we live. But *we* know where he lives. Come on!"

They ran all the way from the field to Bobby's house. Marci raced up the front steps to ring the doorbell.

There was no answer.

"He's just got to be here," Marci said, ringing the bell again.

But no one came to the door.

Marci kept ringing. "Where else can he be?" she wondered aloud.

"Maybe he tried to backtrack with Tiny and find us?" Nicole suggested.

"Then we should have met them," said Carrie.

"Anyway," Annie pointed out, "the woman with the groceries said they were headed for the field."

"Maybe Bobby waited there. Then, when we didn't come, he started looking for us," Marci said.

"But the lady in the garden only saw them once—heading for the field."

"Maybe they took a different route." But even as Marci said that, she didn't believe it. "No, that's stupid. He would have no hope of meeting us, then." She pushed her glasses up on her nose, trying to think. "So where can Bobby and Tiny be?" She looked at her watch. "We're running out of time. The dog show will be starting soon. What are we going to do if we can't find Tiny?"

The other girls had no answer. They stood in silence as Marci tried to come up with some kind of answer.

Marci closed her eyes tight, thinking. As she ran all sorts of thoughts through her mind, she heard something. It was very faint. She wouldn't have heard it at all if everyone hadn't been so quiet. It sounded like . . . whimpering.

She put her hand to her ear and tried to track the sound.

"Marci? What are you doing?" asked Nicole.

"*Sssssshhhhh!*" said Marci. "Don't talk. Just listen!"

"I don't hear anything." Annie shook her head.

Carrie put her hand to her ear. "I do," she said. "Sounds like something crying. Can't you hear it?"

Annie and Nicole listened hard. "You're right!" said Annie.

"I think it's coming from around the back," Nicole added.

They started circling Bobby's house, straining their ears for the whimpering sound.

"Nicole's right," Carrie said. "It's definitely coming from around the back."

Marci opened the gate to the back yard. "Tiny?" she called.

No dog came charging out at them. They came around the house, but the yard was empty.

"I don't understand it," said Marci. "It sounds like Tiny. But it's too soft—kind of muffled."

The girls went quiet again, trying to find where the sound was coming from.

With her head bent to one side, Marci started for the house. "It's getting louder," she whispered.

She passed a basement window. "Louder," she said.

She walked on for a few steps. "Softer," she suddenly said.

Heading back to the window, she got more and more excited. "Louder—louder—*louder!*"

Marci knelt by the window and looked inside.

"Oh, Tiny!" she exclaimed. "What are you doing down there?"

Chapter
7

The girls crowded around the window, peeking inside. The basement looked almost the same as when they had visited. The pool table was right where it had been. Tiny was huddled under it, whimpering.

On one side of the big dog was Bobby's drum set. On the other side was a single snare drum—with a big hole in it.

"Oh, *no!*" Marci gasped. "Tiny broke one of Bobby's drums! What are we going to do?"

She thought for a second. "We've got to get Tiny out, first, and get him to the show. Then we can pay Bobby back from Mr. Jenkins's money."

"Oh, great," said Nicole. "Do you know what one of those drums costs?"

"That's not our problem right now," Annie said.

"We have to figure out how to get in there and get Tiny out. Nobody's home, and the door is locked."

"Wait a second," said Carrie. "Look at this."

She pushed against the basement window. Slowly, it began to open.

"Boy, are we lucky," said Annie.

"Okay, Carrie," Marci said. "Now all you have to do is climb down through there, get Tiny, and take him out through the door."

Carrie turned to her. "How come *I* get that job?" she demanded.

"Well, this will mean climbing, and you're the most athletic," Marci said. "Not to mention that you'd be the easiest to get through the window. . . ."

"I don't care," said Carrie. "No way am I going into that basement alone."

Marci looked at Annie and Nicole. But they both looked away. "All right." She sighed. "*I'll* go with you. But you have to go first."

Carrie opened the window as wide as she could. She got down on the ground and crawled backward until her feet were through the opening. Then she lay down and swung her long legs. A second later, only her hands were on the window ledge. Then she dropped out of sight.

The next thing they heard was a loud sneeze. "I'm covered with dust, but I'm in!" Carrie called, stepping back so the others could see her. "Now you!"

Marci sighed as she got on her hands and knees. "I just hope I fit," she muttered, crawling backward.

"What a time to be wearing shorts." Her feet were through, just hanging in open air. She wiggled back, and her bottom hit the top of the window. Surprised, she jumped—and her knee slipped off the window ledge.

"WhoooooooooooaAAAAAAHHHHH!" Marci said as she began to slide down, waving her arms and legs wildly.

Suddenly, somebody grabbed one of her legs. "Get your hands on that window ledge," Carrie commanded.

Marci grabbed the sides of the window as Carrie helped lower her down.

"Okay, you've got maybe a foot to drop. Let go of the window now."

Marci let go and landed on the basement floor. "Ow!" she said, rubbing her knee. "Oh, look, I scraped it on that stupid windowsill."

Tiny was dancing all around them, waving his stubby tail and whining excitedly.

"Well, you're glad to see us," Marci said. She knelt down and patted Tiny's head. "Easy, boy," she said. "Take it easy."

Tiny whined some more and licked her hand. But he sat down and got quiet.

"There, now," Marci said. "Let's get hold of his collar. We'll get him up these stairs, into the kitchen, then out the front door."

They were just heading up the stairs when Nicole

called to them from the window. "Marci!" she hissed. "There's a car pulling in front of the house!"

Marci, Carrie, and Tiny froze as they heard the front door opening. Above their heads, they could hear footsteps and the sounds of grown-ups talking.

"It must be Bobby's parents," Marci whispered. "But I don't hear Bobby with them."

"What are we going to do?" Carrie whispered back.

"Go back down," Marci answered.

Careful to make no noise, they led Tiny back to the pool table.

"We can't just come walking into their kitchen with Tiny," Marci said. "Bobby's parents will think we broke in here."

"We *did!*" Carrie said nervously. "Maybe we can climb out, ring their bell, and say we heard Tiny whimpering."

"Yeah," said Marci. "I can see us now. 'We just happened to be in your back yard and heard our dog in your basement.' " She shook her head. "Besides, what about Bobby's broken drum? Once they see that, we'll never get out of here. We'll miss the dog show for sure."

She looked from Tiny to the window. "There's only one way I can see."

Carrie stared at her friend. "You can't be serious," she said.

Marci only nodded, and a few moments later, they were working together, trying to hoist Tiny to the window.

The big dog whined in confusion, not understanding what was going on.

"Hush, Tiny," Marci gasped. "We just have to lift a little more. Annie, Nicole, you'll have to help grab him . . . *Ooof!*"

Suddenly, Carrie, Marci, and Tiny tumbled to the floor. Tiny almost barked, but Marci got her hand around his mouth. They lay there frozen for a second, sure that the McCanns had heard something.

But the talking went on upstairs as if nothing had happened.

Groaning under their breath, Carrie and Marci got to their feet.

"Well, we'll just have to try again," Marci puffed.

But their muscles were too tired. They couldn't even lift Tiny near the window. Carrie and Marci sat down against the wall, trying to get their strength back.

"It's too bad Tiny just sits there on us," Marci said. "He's so heavy."

"He just doesn't understand what we want him to do," Carrie said, patting Tiny on the head.

"If we only had some way of making him want to get out that window, he would help us." Marci shook her head. "But how can we do that?"

A funny expression came over Carrie's face as she reached into her pocket. "I think I've got a way," she said.

Her hand came out of her pocket with a wrapped doggy treat. "You feel ready to try again?" she asked Marci.

"Let's do it!" Marci said.

Carrie reached up on tiptoes. "Hey, you guys," she whispered to Annie and Nicole. "Open this up. When we say, 'Ready,' poke it through the window."

Together, she and Marci picked up Tiny for the third time. They brought him as close to the window as they could. Then they both said, "Ready!"

Nicole's hand poked through the window with the doggy treat.

Tiny took one look and one sniff. Then he lunged for the window. Marci and Carrie staggered as he jumped. But Tiny had both his forepaws on the windowsill. His rear legs scratched against the basement wall, trying to push him up.

"Take his legs—take his legs!" Marci commanded, grabbing one of Tiny's legs. Pushing off against her, he gained another inch or two through the window. Annie grabbed one of his forelegs and pulled. Tiny dug with his paws into the ground, trying to hoist himself forward. Carrie and Marci pushed from behind. Tiny moved forward, moved forward, and then . . . "

"He's stuck!" Nicole hissed. "Now what are we supposed to do?"

"Whatever you do, don't let him bark!" Marci said, ducking Tiny's flailing legs. She thought for a moment. "Nicole!" she called as loudly as she dared. "Stick the doggy treat right in front of his nose, but out of his reach, okay?"

"Okay," said Nicole dubiously.

She put the treat right in front of Tiny's nose.

Down in the basement, Carrie and Marci braced themselves under Tiny's feet.

Tiny's ears went back. With a growl, he squirmed himself forward toward the treat.

Then, with a sudden rush, he was through the window!

"Ooooof!" Marci and Carrie heard through the window. "Get him off me!"

Then Carrie and Marci heard footsteps heading toward the basement. "Bobby?" they heard a voice call. "Was that you?"

The two girls stared at each other in panic.

"Come on," Carrie said, giving Marci a boost.

Marci frantically wriggled through the window. Then she turned around to offer Carrie a hand.

Just as Marci, Annie, and Nicole pulled Carrie through the window, they heard a voice from the top of the stairs. "Who's down here?"

They didn't stay to hear anything else. Grabbing Tiny's collar, they dashed for the back-yard gate.

Chapter **8**

Annie glanced over her shoulder as the Super Squad ran down the street with Tiny.

"I guess they didn't see anyone at the window," she said. "Nobody's coming after us."

"Save your breath for running." Marci gulped air. "We still have to get Tiny home and ready for the show."

Marci looked down at her watch. No one said anything out loud, but she knew they all had the same thought. How would they get to the dog show on time?

Mr. Jenkins was pacing back and forth on his porch as they came running through his garden gate. "Tiny!" the old man said, a smile lighting up his features.

Tiny gave a joyful bark and climbed the steps to lick his master's hand.

"Let's get going," Marci said. "Annie, Nicole, get the tub. Carrie, get the bucket. I'll get the hose. Tiny really needs a bath now."

Poor Tiny certainly did. Besides grass stains and dirt from his run, he had dust all over him from climbing out of the basement.

The girls braced themselves for a major fight when they had the tub filled, but Tiny seemed eager to please. He climbed into the tub with only a little urging.

"It's almost as though he knows how important all this is," Carrie said.

They quickly scrubbed Tiny down, then rinsed him off.

"He looks like a new dog," Annie said as she came forward with a towel. "Now, step out of the tub, Tiny. And no shaking this time!"

The big, dripping dog quietly got out of the tub and walked toward Annie. "That's a good dog," she said, starting to wrap the towel around him.

Just then, Nicole came running from the house. "We're in luck!" she said. "Mr. Jenkins got one of these for his birthday last year!"

With one hand, she was unreeling an extension cord. In the other, she held an electric blow dryer. "This will get Tiny dried in no time!"

She turned on the dryer, which made a loud whirring noise as it blew hot air.

Tiny jumped forward—right into Annie.

"*Glub!*" she said as she toppled backward, buried by the wet dog.

Carrie and Marci moved to get Tiny off Annie. They held him down as Annie and Nicole started drying him off.

After Tiny calmed down, he even seemed to enjoy the warm air blowing on him.

Annie got out her special brushes and set to work grooming Tiny's coat. "How much time have we got left?" she asked as she brushed.

Marci looked at her watch. "Not much," she said.

Just as Annie finished the job, Mr. Jenkins appeared on the porch. He had changed into a suit and carried a brand-new leash for Tiny. "Clip this onto his collar," he said, giving the leash to Marci. "I'll bring the car around."

The girls climbed into Mr. Jenkins's station wagon. Marci and Annie sat in the back with Tiny. They looked anxiously at their watches as they drove to the fairgrounds.

Mr. Jenkins made it just before the starting time for the Riverview Dog Show.

The girls spilled out of the car, leading Tiny to the large tent where the show took place. Mr. Jenkins stepped along briskly behind them.

They stepped through the entrance, and everything seemed to get quiet for a moment. The tent was full of dogs—and people—all decked to the nines.

And everyone was staring at the Super Squad. And they were some sight to see. Carrie still had dust from the basement windowsill in her hair. Nicole had grass stains from where Tiny had knocked her down on the McCanns' lawn. Marci had her scraped knee. And Annie was still dripping from Tiny's bath.

"Oh, *no!*" said Nicole. "We forgot to change."

"There was no time to change," Marci said.

"Well, at least it's Tiny who's up for the prize," said Carrie. "We're not in the contest—unless they have a prize for messiest-looking helpers."

"We'd better find out where we're supposed to go," said Annie.

Ignoring the stares they were getting, they quickly passed a line of dogs, each one barking his head off. "That must be the Loudest Dog contest," Annie said. "I saw it in the catalogue."

Next came a line of weird-looking (or weird-acting) dogs. The girls looked at Annie. "Funniest Dog, I guess." She shrugged.

Mr. Jenkins finally asked a man with a badge on his chest that read "Judge."

"Most Beautiful Dog?" the judge said, looking through a bunch of papers. "Aisle Three. Not many dogs in that contest."

They hurried over to Aisle Three and found that the judge was right. There were only four or five other contestants. "Mr. Jenkins?" another judge said, checking Tiny's name on his list. "Just in time."

The first contestant marched out. It was a Pekingese, led by a lady with a little, round, squinched-up face.

"She looks just like her dog," Nicole whispered.

Ms. Pekingese led her dog around, then said, "Now, Tiddles, your trick."

"Trick?" said Marci.

"*Shhh!*" said the judge. "Every entry must perform a trick."

The Squad members all looked at each other. "A trick?" they whispered.

They watched as Tiddles the Pekingese walked on her hind legs to a smattering of applause.

The second owner wore a black suit. He had a thin face with a long nose. So did his dog, a Russian wolfhound.

Dog and owner marched around. Then the owner clapped his hands. His wolfhound rolled over and played dead.

"Very good," said the judge. He turned to Mr. Jenkins. "Your turn."

Mr. Jenkins led Tiny out.

"They look good," Marci whispered. "Very good."

But when the judge asked about a trick, Mr. Jenkins looked puzzled. "Oh, er . . . yes," he said. "Er, Tiny . . . Sit!"

Tiny sat. "Is that all?" a voice came from the crowd.

Mr. Jenkins walked away from Tiny. "Come," he called.

Tiny came.

"Yeah? And?" said the voice.

"He's going to lose," Annie whispered.

"No, he's not," Nicole whispered back. She raised her voice. "Hey, Tiny!"

Tiny's ears perked up. Then he turned a perfect somersault.

Everyone clapped. Mr. Jenkins looked astounded.

"Very good," said the judge. "And now, for the next contestant . . ."

Marci gasped when the next dog marched out. She knew that dog—Bucky, the Chihuahua. And she glared at the boy in the suit holding Bucky's leash.

"*Now* I know why Tiny was locked up in the cellar!" she said. "To keep him out of Bucky's way!"

Chapter 9

"Bobby McCann!" Marci marched over to him. "What do you think you're doing?"

Bobby stared at her. "I'm showing my dog. And you're stopping me right in the middle of it."

"I ought to punch you right in the middle of your nose," Marci said. "You stole Tiny and locked him up so your dog could win the show!"

It would have sounded a lot better if Bucky hadn't come jumping at her. *"Ra-ra-ra-ra-RA!!!"* shrieked the little dog, nipping at Marci's ankles. She was so busy jumping around, she almost didn't hear what Bobby was saying.

"I don't know what you're talking about!" His blue eyes were frosty.

"I do," said a voice. Tommy Mills came out of the

crowd. He hung his head. "Bobby had nothing to do with it. I stole your dog. When we met in the field, you mentioned Mr. Jenkins's name. I looked him up in the phone book and got his address. Early this morning, I went over to his house. There was Tiny, sitting out in the yard. He knew me. So it was easy to take his collar and lead him off for a walk."

"But why?" Marci and Bobby asked together.

Tommy shook his head. "I was afraid Tiny would beat Bucky. Bobby really needs the prize money—it's a hundred dollars. The day after we met you, his snare drum broke during practice. We need one for the dance tonight, but none of us has any money. Bobby was counting on winning the prize to pay for a new drum."

He looked up. "I did it for the band. I was desperate."

Marci watched as Bobby bit his lip. "You must have been crazy," he said.

"Why did you hide Tiny in Bobby's house?" Marci wanted to know.

"My family lives in an apartment—so I couldn't hide him there. I knew that Bobby's folks wouldn't be home in the morning—and he lent me his keys."

"You were supposed to bring your amp over and leave it in the basement. Instead you brought Tiny over?" Bobby said.

"I'm sorry it happened," Tommy said. "Could you ever forgive me, Bobby?" Then he looked over at Nicole. "Could *you* forgive me?"

"I'm just glad we happened to find Tiny," Nicole said.

"I'm also glad Tiny wasn't the one who broke that drum," Marci added.

"Well, I'm glad we managed to get Tiny to lose some weight," Carrie called out. "Otherwise, we'd never have gotten him through that window."

Marci had to giggle at that.

Then the judge came marching over. "What is going on here?" he demanded.

That was the last straw for Bucky. With a shrill *"Ra-ra-ra-ra-RA!"* she lunged for the judge.

"That dog is off its lead!" the judge said, dodging back. "I'm disqualifying him from this contest."

"Oh, *no!*" said Bobby.

"After him!" yelled Marci.

The Squad members plus Bobby and Tommy set off in pursuit. It was a short chase, really. They always knew where Bucky was. It just meant looking for the place with the loudest noise and the most confusion.

People were jumping around, and the dogs were going nuts. Some were barking enough to get into the Loudest Dog contest. Others were trying to chase Bucky. They could have made it to the finals for Funniest Dog, tripping their owners and barking their heads off.

They finally managed to corner Bucky under the registration table. While Bobby picked Bucky up, Annie was quickly paging through a show catalogue.

"I thought I remembered seeing it in here," she said. Finally, she pointed at a page. "Here it is. You're in the right place to sign up, and this contest hasn't even started yet."

Marci read the name of the contest. "Annie!" she cried, "you're a genius!"

A little while later, the judge was making his announcement. "For our Smallest Dog contest, the winner is"—he shuffled his papers importantly— "Bucky, owned by Mr. McCann."

Bobby smiled as the man put the blue ribbon in his hand.

But Bobby's smile got bigger as the judge handed him an envelope. "One hundred dollars in prize money. Congratulations, young man. Now I have another contest to judge."

"I can get my snare drum," Bobby said, smiling at Marci. "How can I ever thank you?" He leaned over and gave her a big hug.

Marci turned bright red. She didn't know what to say.

"Just play well tonight," Nicole said. "Remember, we'll all be there watching."

Bobby grinned. "You can bet on it," he said. "And remember, we'll all be watching for you!"

He went over and gathered up Bucky. "And now, it's time for us to go. I've got to see a man about a drum." Bobby and Tommy waved good-bye.

Marci, Nicole, and the other Squad members waved back.

"Girls! Girls!" they heard a voice calling from behind them.

"Oh, no!" said Marci. "We completely forgot about Mr. Jenkins!"

They turned to see Mr. Jenkins waving frantically at them. He led Tiny on his leash. And pinned on Tiny's collar was a big blue ribbon. Tiny walked along proudly, enjoying the attention he was getting from everyone at the show.

"I had a hard time finding you, after you rushed off with those young men," Mr. Jenkins said. "We still have business to attend to. I was supposed to pay you when you had Tiny ready for the show. But we were in rather a hurry then, and I forgot. So, here is your payment." He pulled out a check, which he handed to Marci.

"Well, thanks, Mr. Jenkins. We—"

But Mr. Jenkins wasn't finished. "And I'd like to give you *this* as a bonus."

He handed Marci the judge's envelope with the prize money—a crisp hundred-dollar bill.

"B-But Mr. Jenkins," she sputtered, "we can't take this. You won it."

Mr. Jenkins shook his head. "My dears, *you* won it, with all your hard work. I have what I want."

He reached down to fondle the blue ribbon for a second. Then he patted Tiny on the head. "With your help, I showed that my Tiny is still a winner."

Chapter **10**

"Well, here we are." Mr. Arnold brought the car to a stop in front of the school. "Have a good time at the dance, sweetheart. Remember to give me a call when you want to come home."

"Thanks, Dad," said Marci. She got out of the car, and her father took off. She stood by the street, waving, until he turned a corner and was out of sight.

Marci turned toward the school, wishing for the fifteenth time that she could just have gone with her friends. But no, her dad had insisted on "playing chauffeur," as he called it. At least he hadn't worn his old cab-driver's hat as he had threatened.

A group of older girls came down the street and went into the school, laughing loudly.

"Loud Noise is playing tonight!" one girl said. "I can hardly wait to see them. That Bobby McCann is so cute!"

Marci turned and looked up the block, pretending to be looking for someone. She didn't want those girls to see how pink her cheeks had gotten.

She looked at her watch. It was still too early to go in. Nobody she knew would be in there.

She glanced down at the clothes she was wearing. Had she made a mistake, choosing this outfit? She tugged on her new red dress. Was it too short? Was it not short enough?

A car pulled up, and Annie Lewis popped out the door. "Thanks for the lift, Dad!" she called out. She closed the door, and the car pulled away.

"Hey, Marci," Annie said as she saw her friend. "Did you just get here?"

"Uh, yeah," said Marci. "Your father drove you over, too?"

Annie nodded. "You'd think I had never gone to a dance before." She giggled, then glanced over at the school door. "So, do you want to go in?"

"Oh, I thought I would wait for a minute," Marci said.

"You want to get ready for your entrance," Annie said, her eyes twinkling wickedly. "To make sure Bobby sees you."

Marci could feel her cheeks turning pink again. "Cut it out, Annie."

90

"Aw, come on," Annie said. "We're going to have fun tonight."

"I hope so," said Marci.

Another car came to a stop. The door opened, and out came Carrie and Nicole.

"Hi, kids," said Carrie.

"My father wanted to drive me over," Nicole said, rolling her eyes. "*Honestly*. But I managed to get a lift with Carrie, instead." She was wearing her hair high on her head and gave it a careful pat. Long silver earrings dangled from her ears.

But Annie was looking down at Carrie's feet. "New shoes?" she asked, pointing at the shiny black T-straps.

"Yeah." Carrie shifted her feet uncomfortably. "I wish I could have worn my running shoes, instead."

"Well, we're all here," said Annie.

"Yeah," said Marci in a faint voice.

"Let's go in." Nicole's eyes sparkled with excitement, and her earrings jingled musically. "I can hardly wait to see Tommy."

"Yeah." Marci's voice was even fainter.

They walked through the doors and bought their tickets. Then they headed for the gym. All along the hallway, crepe-paper streamers were hung, and the gym doors were covered with crepe-paper bows. They could hear the buzz of kids talking and loud laughter. And under that was the muffled sound of music.

When they opened the gym doors, the music came

91

blasting out. Loud Noise was living up to its name. They were playing a loud, fast song, and lots of kids were dancing.

The band was on a stage set up in the front part of the gym, with spotlights shining down. The rest of the gym was lit more dimly. Even at this distance, Marci could see Bobby clearly, pounding out the beat on his drums. Joe and Dennis were rocking with their guitars, and Tommy was hunched over his keyboard, wailing away.

"Lucky thing we didn't bring Tiny with us," Carrie said. "He'd be howling his head off."

"Doesn't Tommy look hot?" Nicole asked. "Let's get closer."

They worked their way along the side of the gym, away from the dancers.

Marci's heart began to sink when she saw the big crowd in front of the stage. Lots of people were just standing there, listening to the music. We'll never get through, she thought.

But she hadn't counted on Nicole Tucker. With an "Excuse me," a couple of "Pardon me's," and a good pair of elbows, Nicole cut a path for them.

Soon, they were in the first row of the crowd. The music was very loud in front of the amplifiers. Marci's whole body seemed to vibrate in time with Dennis's bass.

She watched Bobby's light-brown hair fly down onto his forehead as he played. All his attention was on his drums. Whenever he looked up, it was to glance over at Dennis or Joe. They sounded very good.

Marci also saw the new snare drum. It was the same pattern as the rest of Bobby's set, just a little shinier. He got good use out of his prize money.

Bobby smashed at the cymbals and twirled his drumsticks as the band went into the finale of the song. They played even louder, if that were possible.

Then it was over, and the kids in the front were cheering wildly.

Bobby looked up from his drums and ran his eyes over the crowd. He stopped when he saw Marci, and a big smile came over his face. Standing up, he called Joe, Dennis, and Tommy over. They talked for a moment, then went back to their instruments.

Bobby did a drum roll on his new snare. "We'd like to say a special hello to some friends of ours," he said into his microphone. "Marci Arnold, Carrie Young, Annie Lewis, and Nicole Tucker. Without their help, our drums wouldn't sound so great tonight. I'm glad—we're *all* glad they could make it. So we're going to do a special song for them. It's an oldie, but I'm sure they'll get the joke." Bobby looked at Marci again and grinned.

She grinned back.

Then Bobby turned to the other band members. "Okay," he said. "A-one, two, three!"

With that, Loud Noise began playing, and Tommy began to sing, "You ain't nothin' but a hound dog."

The girls of the Super Squad all looked at each other and laughed.